Sunrise at Deer Camp
Thomas A. Fischer

Copyright © 2020 Tom Fischer

Farm House Books—Madison, WI
ISBN: 978-0-578-70462-3
Library of Congress Control Number: 2020910297
Title: Sunrise at Deer Camp
Author: Thomas Fischer
Digital distribution | 2020
Paperback | 2020

This is a work of fiction. The characters, names, incidents, places, and dialogue are products of the author's imagination, and are not to be construed as real.

Dedication

To my parents Bob and Judy Fischer.

Chapter One

The pick-up truck's headlight beams bounced slightly and cut through the dark of the cold November night, as TJ took a left onto the small gravel road. He had taken this road countless times.

As he turned, framed for a moment in the glow of the headlights, a white-tail doe flashed across the small road, and behind it was a little 8-point buck. With a steady snow falling around them, they scuttled across the snow-covered, gravel road. He could not imagine a better sight pulling into deer camp.

TJ turned into the dark, snow-covered drive, and the truck rumbled through as he approached the old shack. In the darkness, he could see the silhouette of the shack against the woods, and smoke was puffing out of the stove pipe, a ghostly column of white rising to the stars.

The tires made a crunching sound on the snow as the truck stopped outside the shack. He breathed a sigh of relief. He was there.

He savored this feeling for a moment as he sat behind the wheel of the truck. He shut off the engine, and he took the keys out of the ignition. The warm air that was in the truck began to dissipate quickly. A smile crept over his face. He sat for a moment and through the windshield looked over the shack and the surrounding woodlot, as his eyes became accustomed to the dark.

TJ looked around the truck to see what he would need to bring in. On the passenger seat next to him was a pile of paper and folders from work. Those would be left behind. He grabbed his black fleece that lay next to the pile.

He opened the door of the truck, and he took a step out into the cold night. A cold breeze made him slightly cringe. But he liked it. His breath was frozen white, and it filtered out of him like the smoke out of that shack stove pipe. While it was dark, his eyes continued to adjust, and the shack and woods sprang up around him. A cold breeze came across his face again, and he took a deep breath. He was excited, but a bit forlorn as well.

He threw on his black fleece, zippered it up over a faded, flannel and he headed toward the shack. The warmth of the fleece was just enough for the walk into the shack. He pulled his hat down by the brim as well. The air near the shack was ripe with the aroma of the smoke from the wood burning stove. With each step, his boots crunched and squeaked over the snow.

The door handle to the shack was quite cold, a mild, cold burn radiated in his palm, but he turned the knob and quickly stepped in. This very moment is what he had been waiting for over the past year.

The warmth of the shack came over him like a wave, and the soft glow of the lights welcomed him along with a big "Hello!" from his father sitting at the table, as he looked up from an old *Field and Stream* Magazine.

TJ had been waiting a year for that exact moment, and it was as satisfying as ever. It was the eve of the opening day of the Wisconsin Deer Gun Hunt, and excitement was abounding at Deer Camp.

On this night, in Central Wisconsin, a few miles away from the mighty Wolf River, deer camp was happening in a small, cozy shack, silhouetted by a woodlot full of oaks, maples, and pines, with a group of four men that took different roads there that night.

TJ walked into the shack and was also greeted by his brother-in-law.

"TJ!" said his brother-in-law, Marlin. "You made it! How was the drive?" he continued.

"Traffic wasn't too bad. I made pretty good time." TJ said with a smile.

"I saw a buck chasing a doe across the road right before I pulled in," TJ stated with controlled excitement.

Good to hear!" Marlin said.

"It's going to be a good hunt...I can feel it," Marlin stated with questioning confidence. He was usually optimistic, at least the night before anyway.

"When did you get here?" TJ asked.

"About an hour ago. Left work early!" said Marlin

Father got up from his chair and the two shook hands. Father loved this weekend as they all did. He didn't care much about the hunting or shooting, but that he liked his boys being together with him.

Marlin had made it up from Kenosha as he did every year, leaving his little family behind for the weekend at Deer Camp. He worked as a maintenance man for an apartment complex. He married into the family years ago, and he became a welcomed member at deer camp ever since. Just an all-around good guy who would help anyone out when needed. Given this was his big weekend, he was ecstatic it was here. He truly looked forward to this all year long as most gun hunters did.

A couple of handshakes and the offer of a beer, and it all began. They chatted for a while. Typical but expected questions that come every year.

With a pause in the conversation, TJ looked around the old, wooden shack. His eyes were roaming over the walls and shelves, and he noticed some old pictures of old hunts. He reminisced a little longer and he remembered his first time walking into deer camp 25 years ago. It was not the same camp, but one farther north in the big woods of Northern Wisconsin.

It was that weekend, 25 years ago, he fell in love with the hunt. He was 13 years old and his father agreed to take him hunting after a little persuading. One of the things he remembered most was the drive to deer camp. He could remember looking out of the car window at the passing scenes of his home, cities, country, and then the big woods.

He and his father walked into that deer camp, and both were filled with anticipation. That camp was an extended trailer in a wooded lot. He could remember so much of that hunt. TJ would be hunting the big woods with his cousins and uncle. That weekend was most memorable, and a perfect introduction to deer hunting. TJ was hooked.

Over the next 25 years he would only miss one opening weekend, and that was due to his daughter being born. He wouldn't have changed that for anything, as it was worth missing the hunt. That would be the only reason he could see missing Opening Weekend. Of course, he went up the next weekend for a one-day hunt after Thanksgiving that he squeezed in, and he shot a deer anyway.

His mind quickly went back to the present, and the hunt that was upon them. He looked around the shack again, and he noticed the usual furnishings and expected items. In the background, *The Second Week of Deer camp* played on the old-timey radio.

The poker cards were on the old wooden table, a bowl of unshelled peanuts next to them, along with some scattered peanut shells around the bowl. A couple half-full beer bottles befriending the peanuts, and the aroma of the wood stove was always a pleasant constant in the background.

TJ stood and talked, and then said, "I need to get my gear from the truck."

He walked out knowing that they were still one man short. His brother would be joining them, but when was the question he thought to himself? He also knew his father would be asking that same question at any moment. He walked with continual anticipation toward the truck.

TJ got to the truck and opened the passenger-side door. The door gave way after the initial tug broke the cold hold that was held on the door. He reached in, and his hand found a travel bag of clothes, bags of food for the week, a bin of hunting equip/clothes, and the shotgun. These all needed to find their way into the shack.

His fingers were getting cold since he did not bother with gloves, and he felt the cold run through his fingers as he closed the door of the truck. The air from his mouth continued to freeze as it left his mouth, flowing in a steady rhythm. He planned for this to be his last trip to the truck for the night, and he walked quickly into the shack.

As soon as he walked back in "When is your brother Pete coming?!" said father.TJ gave a little smile.

He gave him the usual answer, "I'm not sure. He said about 8 o'clock, but who really knows."

In the past, his brother Pete has shown up on time, at midnight, or at 5 am opening morning. Each deer camp had someone like that to be sure. You just never knew what to expect from him.

Father said, "Want a beer?"

TJ smiled and nodded as they all ended up meeting now at the table. The table sat four, but they knew that last seat would be empty for a while.

"Bring your money?" Father asked, as he handed TJ a cold bottle of beer.

"Yep," TJ twisted the bottle cap off the bottle, and he tossed it on the table. He grabbed the cards and began shuffling them.

"Five-card draw deuces are wild." He declared

The beer was cold and washed down the peanuts very well. Peanut shells lay surrounding the bowl in which the peanuts were held. It was a small bowl, faded and yellow.

This deer camp has always played poker, unlike the boys up in Florence, who played Sheepshead, and the hunters up in Escanaba who played Euchre. This camp has always played poker, and that never seemed like it would change.

This would go on for the next couple of hours, and this is generally where the day's stories would be retold, and stories from the past rekindled.

Beer bottles were tilted up, and heads tilted back. Peanut shells occasionally fell to the cement floor, and laughter and good cheer filled the small, red shack. It was the night before the opening morning of a Wisconsin Gun Deer Season, and similar happenings were taking place throughout Wisconsin on the cold November Night. Some would hunt only the weekend, while others would stay on the entire week as well. For many this time is about family and friends, and just getting away more than anything else.

Most of this group had been hunting for a long time, and taken their share of deer, but they weren't always lucky. Father had not shot a deer in many, many years and only made a minimal effort to do so. He wanted to be with his boys and fellow hunters more than anything. Of course, Father was the first one in camp to ever take a deer. That happened over 25 years ago in Antigo.

For some hunters, it was only about shooting a deer. For TJ it was a combination. He loved the cards, and conversation, and family bonding, but deep down he was there to hunt. He loved it. He loved the woods, the wildlife, the weather, and the excitement that overcame him when he was on stand and seeing deer. There was no equivalent. A successful hunt also meant venison for the family.

Their deer camp beginnings started in Antigo, Wisconsin. At that time, it was only father and TJ, and the hunting crew of Antigo. This was his dad's brother's camp.

But prior to that, at the age of 12, he watched his uncles and cousins hunt the farm while visiting over Thanksgiving weekend. As TJ and his Father pulled up to grandpa's drive, he could see his uncles and cousins throughout the property standing out in their blaze orange parkas and the hats. As he watched the fields where his uncles were hunting, two does ran out of some cover and across the field! Shots rang out! The does continued running into an adjacent woodlot. TJ was hooked.

So, he took his hunter safety course through its local school and his father took him hunting, rejoining an already proven hunting camp at his uncle's property. Father and son will join his father's brother and his three boys of adult age. They stayed in an old trailer mobile home.

Giant pine trees, and strong rivers flowed through huge ridges. This was a great inauguration into the deer hunting tradition that he would never forget. The next day he would fire his shotgun at a deer, but he would not connect. By simply taking the shot, he connected to a life that he would grow to love.

His father shot a deer that weekend of hunting in Antigo, and that started the tradition of success at deer camp. That tradition would move to deer camp just 2 hours southeast of Antigo, in south central Wisconsin. The traditions learned at that first deer camp carried over to the next and some new traditions were made as well.

That night they continued to play cards with the radio playing in the background. The *Thirty-Point Buck* song came on and the group was pleased. They sang along. Smiles and a little laughter erupted from time to time.

In the moment, they aren't thinking about how special it all was, but simply getting lost in the moment. TJ looked around the cabin walls.

Chapter 2

The night was rolling on, when they heard a faint sound of a vehicle roll up outside the shack. They assumed it was their long, lost brother Pete, but it wasn't.

It was an uncle on mother's side. He hunted the same family property, but up the road a bit. He was a good-old guy. He lived in an old farmhouse up the road. He was stopping in to see how things were, and where they were all hunting the next day, and for a beer of course.

It was usual for him to stop in the night before the hunt, but you could tell there was an added excitement to his face.

"You won't believe what I just saw!" His glasses were shining in the light from the naked light bulb above the entryway of the shack.

"I was pulling out of the farmhouse and as the headlights hit the cut corn field next to the house, there was a giant buck right there in the middle of my headlights!" Uncle said.

"It was on the edge of the field right next to the farmhouse!" he exclaimed.

With so many buck sightings already, they wondered if they were catching the tail end of the rut.

The other hunters' eyes widened, and their souls leapt with excitement. That was two good luck signs in one night. They couldn't wait for opening morning. Uncle continued to describe the buck. "It was a heavy, dark racked 9 or 10 point with a nice spread. It was huge!" he exclaimed.

"Big buck, looked to be 300 pounds," he said.

Uncle had been known to exaggerate things, but at the same time that size buck definitely could be found in the area. Uncle had taken one 40 years before, right in that same area, and frequently reminded them all of it.

"I haven't seen a buck that big since the one I shot 40 years ago!"

"That didn't take long," the other men thought.

He loved to tell that story.

Uncle went on to share the story of that buck he shot 40 years ago, as he had done many times in the past, and as usual the others listened intently, as it was a great story. This seemed to be the short version. He sat down, and he was handed a bottle of cold beer as he finished up the story.

After that, he kept on talking about the heavy rack on the buck he just saw in the cut corn field just down the road from the shack. They eventually moved off the topic of the buck, and they discussed where they may be hunting in the morning.

"Well I guess I gotta go. Good luck tomorrow," said Uncle.

"Alright, good luck to you too." said TJ

"Thanks for the beer!" Uncle shouted as he slammed the heavy door to the shack.

It seemed like every few years one of these big bucks popped up on the property during the gun season.

Unfortunately, it also seemed that they failed to connect with getting the big bucks. TJ and the boys had taken their share of bucks and does. But those successful years seem to be few and far between for him these days. TJ was looked upon as the better hunter of this deer camp, but his confidence and luck had been wavering these last few years. Life had not been going his way.

They all gathered for a while near the table, and when Uncle headed out it was 9:07 pm. Still waiting for Pete. No concern was on the hunter's faces, as they knew he would be there when he intended to be.

The night moved on, and another classic deer camp song came on the old radio.

A couple of the guys sang along under the breaths a bit.

The wood furnace was dying down, so Father grabbed another piece of wood and set it in the stove. The wood stove was set up near one of the walls, a few steps from the wooden table they played cards at. Across from the table, was an old cast iron sink. They did get running water into the shack after years of only having an outdoor hand-pump.

The inside of the shack was what one might call rustic, and had a "rustic" smell to go with it. The frame was 2x4's and it showed. It literally showed. They never put any paneling up. It was built the same year TJ was born.

Sitting at the table you could look around and see photographs from the past. Old hunts and family vacations. A few sets of antlers on the wall. One was

TJ's first 8 point he shot many years ago. For TJ it was about remembering the hunt. Each set of antlers, like an old photograph, allows one to relive or remember a time from the past. It wasn't about showing them off, unless in a fun way, to remind other hunters of past skill. Otherwise it was about the memory of the hunt. At least for TJ it was.

The shack had several sets of antlers on the wall, and one head mount. Most were TJ's. He loved to sit in the quiet and scan the room. When he looked at a set of antlers on the wall at the shack, he simply found himself back in the woods...the buck walking on the edge of the field, his tree-stand wavering in the wind. The excitement that came across him. The happiness of his fellow hunters as they walked to the deer. Whether looking at a three-point rack or the heavy, dark rack of an 8 pt he shot one year, it was the same feeling.

On the walls alongside the antlers, were old wood or tin signs for Jim Beam Bourbon Whiskey, Remington firearms, giving the little shack some hunting character. Above the propane powered stove is a row of pots and pans hanging from a row of nails. They cluttered and clanked with any movement around them it seemed. Everything was second hand from mom's kitchen or from the local rummage sales.

On the other side of the room were wooden bunks. They were made years ago, they would be finding themselves making our way to them soon, as the nightly cheer was for the most part winding down. The floor of the shack was cement, and in a few select places it was covered with some second-hand rugs.

Very soon the question of where everyone would hunt tomorrow would come up. It was all private land owned by the family or extended family. The land was a combination of hardwoods, swamp, farm fields, pine rows and a creek bottom. It all was a part of four different areas known to these hunters as Fathers Woods, the Farm, Maggie's, and the Creek Bottom.

Chapter 3

Father's woods were the acreage around the shack. This woodlot was filled with tall, beautiful maples and oaks for the most part. The south end of the property had a gradual, small ridge that ran the length of it. A somewhat circular trail ran through these woods. Father's stand was only about 100 yards away, and that's how he liked it. His time on stand was getting shorter each year, but the hunting was not the main reason he took part in this old tradition that goes back to the Oneida Nation; he took part in it to be with his boys. Father's woodlot was connected to the Farm property, but a small gravel road split the two.

The Farm was where a good deal of hunting had taken place over the years, and in the heart of that property is where the biggest bucks were taken. It was made up of tree lines near corn or bean fields, along with a small swamp in the middle of the property, and it was a half mile from the deer shack. This was owned by Uncle. 100 acres of prime hunting land. The Farm was known for producing the biggest bucks. TJ had shot quite a few of them. His favorite area to hunt was the middle of the swamp. This was the darkest, thickest part of the property where the big bucks felt safe. Most hunters stayed on the edge of the swamp, not willing to deal with the wet, thick, and rugged terrain. Many a hunting story takes place in the swamp. Hits and misses alike.

Maggie's land was owned by one of their aunts and she allowed them, and them only, to hunt it during the gun season. This property was next to the Farm, and about 40 acres. They were always grateful to her and uncle for allowing them to hunt this land. Whenever they took deer off their properties, they always shared it with them. Maggie's land was mainly open crop fields with tree lines throughout, but it also connected them to the creek bottom.

The Creek Bottom was family land as well, and the terrain shifted greatly here. From Maggie's land it dropped sharply, and the creek bottom had a good-sized, strong creek running through it, and was up to eight feet deep in certain areas where the water hit the banks hard and fast. On the south side of this property was a pine ridge, and throughout the middle was marshy land, and thick brush near the creek. Several good bucks, and a lot of deer were seen here as well. The creek bottom was about a mile away from deer camp.

The tricky part about this property was that the creek split it in half and you could only get across using the Tree Bridge; otherwise one would have to drive around to the other side, and come in from the road. The Tree bridge was solid, but the footing could be tricky, and it leaned over one of the deepest parts of the creek. They could not remember when the big oak had fallen over, but it seemed like it was always there.

While it seemed to be there for many, many years, there were no signs of rot or deterioration which seemed odd. TJ crossed this bridge fifty times probably over the years, and had never fallen into the creek below, even when it was icy, or snow covered. He had a few close calls, but never went in.

The card game finished up, and it was getting late. Father headed off to his bunk, and TJ began to think about when his brother Pete would get there as he slid the deck of cards back in its sleeve. Marlin and TJ left the table and were tending to gear that they would be using the next day... blaze orange parkas, Sorel boots, shotgun slugs, binoculars, and hand warmers. Everything laid out and ready for the next morning's hunt.

A quiet excitement came over the shack that one could feel. Each of them focused more on making sure they were ready when all of a sudden, the door opened wide and with the frigid late-night air, entered Pete. His distinct graying, fully grown and long goatee, and balding head made his way into the shack.

"Ready to hunt!?" he shouted.

"Close the door!" They all yelled at him

He of course purposely left it open a little longer than he needed to, making sure they all felt the chill, but then slammed it closed. Marlin and TJ were very happy to see him. Each of the fellas brought their personalities to deer camp, and Pete always kept everyone laughing.

You could feel the cold coming off him even from a few feet away. This was a colder than normal year, yet not the coldest. Pete made his way to the furthest bunk in the back corner of the shack and put down his gear. This was his spot and that seemed like it would never change. As he walked back toward the

17

woodstove, TJ handed him a beer, and Pete guzzled it down. He had a long drive.

"It's cold out there," was muttered behind a tilted back beer bottle.

TJ recalled one year when they woke up to 10-degree temps, and they all walked in from the morning hunt with ice layered into their beards. That opening weekend they spent more time in the shack than in their deer stands. It was that cold.

Pete was TJ's elder by 10 years and 20 pounds, and one of TJ's closest friends. They were all there at this point. Life was good. Tomorrow was opening day. The three grown men all stood in a circle with schoolboy smiles running across their faces. Father was already snoring in bed.

It was getting late, and Pete was tired from his drive. Before he headed to the bunk, TJ slipped outside one last time. The cold encapsulated him immediately as he closed the heavy shack door. He moved away from the shack a bit and looked up to the stars. They were shining so bright. No city lights to buffer the brightness, just a cold, dark sky, and a million little twinkling stars above in the sky.

A cold breeze made his eyes water and skin tingle. He loved that feeling. He took a few deep breaths and looked at the woods. The night was quiet except for the wind. The wind and the whiskey made him lose his footing a little, but he quickly regained his footing, gave a smile, took a deep breath, and walked back into the shack.

As he slipped into his sleeping bag in his bunk, other thoughts crept into his mind. He wondered how his children were doing a couple hundred miles away.

They would be staying with their mother while he hunted. He laid there and thought of each one of them, and how much He loved them and how wonderfully unique each one was.

Coincidently, they all enjoyed the outdoors. They fished, hiked, and camped together. He loved them so much. He hoped they knew that. He told them that a lot, but he hoped they knew how he truly meant it. They got him through the hard times. His thoughts slipped back to the upcoming hunt.

A small smile crossed his face as his eyes began to close, and sleep came over him. The last sound he heard was Pete putting wood into the fire and the closing of the metal door. A quiet metal to metal grating sound filled the quiet void of the shack. You could still hear the fire hiss, pop, and crackle. As that happened, a shrinking aroma of burning wood filled the shack. He drifted off to sleep.

Chapter 4

TJ awoke to Pete sawing logs a couple of bunks over. It was like a freight train was coming through the shack. TJ turned over in his sleeping bag trying to find the last bit of warmth, and to hide his ears from the monstrous snoring.

At this point of the morning, the fire in the wood furnace was merely glowing embers. A cold came over the shack that seemed to hurt as they left their sleeping bags. The floor of the shack was cement with a few well-placed rugs spread throughout. Even with the rugs, the cold quickly crept up from the floor to the soles of their feet

Father yelled from his bunk "Throw some wood in the fire!"

TJ headed toward the crate of wood near the wood furnace. Even with wool socks on, his feet felt the bitter cold floor with each step he took, and it seemed to make its way up his legs. He set the wood in the stove, and he fired it up. He stretched in the dark of that morning, and he thought to himself, it is Opening Day. A heartfelt smile came over his face. It was 4:44 am.

Everyone else was still in their bunks. Some were snoring, the others were moaning and groaning a bit.

"Start the coffee," came from the back corner of the shack.

TJ, already heading toward the coffee pot, walked over to the coffee pot that he got ready the night before, and he flipped the switch. Soon it came alive with some hissing noises, and after a little while, hot coffee began to drip.

The aroma of brewing coffee quickly began to fill the room. TJ turned on a light and began sorting out some breakfast items. He opened the pack of donuts, tossed some paper plates onto the table, and breakfast was served. TJ moved to the old radio sitting atop a shelf. Next to the radio was an antler. A small antler shed with 4 points on it. TJ turned the small round knob on the radio, and it clicked and then crackled a bit and the station came clear as he walked away. An old George Jones song was playing.

Opening morning breakfast has always been kept simple at this deer camp. A couple packages of donuts, juice, and coffee generally did the trick. TJ had laid out everything for the others and walked back to the coffee pot. It was half-full and still dripping. The fresh smell of brewing coffee, and the warmth from the woodstove began to slowly flow throughout the shack. Not a lot of warmth, but you could feel it creep over the cold...pushing it toward the walls and ceiling.

TJ began to move a little quicker, as he got some coffee mugs ready, and then he heard someone get out of their bunk and appear out of the darkness and into the dim light. Marlin moved toward the bathroom. In the past they only had the outhouse. Father had really spruced this place up now! The shack was not only used for deer camp, but a summer and fall retreat for the family as well. Father wanted everyone to enjoy it, so he added some comforts that would otherwise not be expected at deer camp.

With some more moaning and groaning, Pete left his bunk, and made his way to the coffee TJ just poured for him. It steamed and added more warmth to the shack as he filled the other two cups. Father continued to sleep. His deer stand was near the shack, while the rest of them had at least a quarter or half mile to walk.

They made their way to the table, and they quietly munched on donuts and sipped hot coffee. The coffee, hot and comforting, was a welcome part of the morning. The powder from the donuts fell to the table or attached to the untrimmed beards. No words were spoken yet, when suddenly the question that had to be asked by someone was asked. Pete looked at TJ and asked, "Where are you hunting?" TJ thought briefly, still waking up, and said "the Swamp"

These questions had to be asked, yet they knew for the most part where they each would be hunting without really asking. For the most they each hunted the same stands each opening morning. Marlin would go to the Box stand overlooking a meadow that was on the outskirts of the swamp. Pete would hunt the back tree line, and TJ would go to the Swamp stand. They would hunt different spots throughout the season, but opening morning would generally find them in their usual haunts.

Father finally came out and joined them at the table. Things were still quiet, each one of them thinking of what he would need for the day...hoping to see deer, hoping for a buck. They also had two doe tags between them.

TJ left the table and went to his gear. He laid it all out on his bunk and looked over. TJ didn't want to bring anything he really didn't need. He layered his clothing and slipped on a new pair off wool socks. The last thing you needed to do before heading out to stand was to get his shotgun out of the case. The morning ritual was in full swing.

Slipping on his boots and tying them tightly. The snugness of the socks and boots felt good and all was feeling right. He was almost ready to head out. They all got ready early as the three of them had longer walks ahead of them. One by one they slipped on the blaze orange parkas and hats. Extra slugs in their pockets, and gloves on their hands they grabbed their shotguns and made their way toward the door.

For the last hour and 15 minutes it has been relatively warm in the shack. That cozy feeling was about to end. TJ opened the door, and the cold November wind hit his face as if he had walked into a wall. It quickly bit their faces and watered their eyes. He zippered up his parka until it hit his chin, and pulled his blaze orange stocking cap down farther. Even as his face burned a bit from the cold, he loved the feeling. It was very cold, but it had been colder on opening mornings of the past. Once you get through that initial greeting from the weather, it is... tolerable. The three of them moved out toward the road. All walking in unison next to each other.

"Good luck," yelled Father.

"You too," quietly yelled Marlin back.

As they left, Willie Nelson quietly sang, *On the Road Again.*

23

They crossed the road and into the open field it was still dark, and no words were spoken. The stars were still in the sky, as it was a good hour before first light. The snow quietly crunched beneath their feet as they made their way forward.

They came to a point where Marlin would break off and would head to the Box Stand. His silhouette disappeared into the nothing. Pete and TJ walked together farther. They were coming up to the tree line stand where Pete would hunt that morning. They parted simply with a quiet "good luck." TJ continued. The swamp stand was in the deepest part of the property.

The North Star still in the sky, led them toward their stands, as he anxiously left the side of Pete, and took a trail around the back of the property. While still in darkness he knew young pine trees and bushes were alongside the trail. His thoughts were on the day to come, and what the sunrise may bring. TJ made it to the swamp stand and quietly climbed the ladder. The wooden ladder groaned and creaked, as he slowly made his ascent to the platform.

TJ got to the top and began to situate himself. He sat down and the stand creaked and groaned a bit in the cold. He felt ready but had some time before first light. He made sure he had everything needed at hand, and then turned his attention to the Winchester, but as he handled it in his hands, his gaze went upward as something caught his eye. The stars still were shining but fading with each passing minute. The sky was clear, stars twinkling.

Then something happened that he never saw before while hunting. As he stared into the dark sky, he saw bright streaks flying across the sky, bright and faded as they fell into the atmosphere. Several more rocketed across the dark sky leaving only a momentary blaze. It was a brilliant display of nature. A little meteor-shower. It was amazing.

The early morning sky came alive, and he watched the brief meteor slowly fizzle away. He had never seen this before. He would never forget it. Most of the experiences gained through hunting having little to do with shooting a deer. With the light show over, his attention went back toward the ground. He always thoroughly enjoyed this time before the dawn and soaked it in as much as he could. He then realized he needed to load his shotgun.

He then waited for the sun to rise as it would bring some warmth to this frigid morning, but he had a good 15 minutes or so before that would happen. As he sat in the stand, he heard a sound to his left. The sound of a deer moving. While this could be a frustrating thing to happen before he could see or even shoot a deer, it was one of his favorite things of the hunt.

It was a deer, but due to the lack of visibility a shot could not be taken. Nonetheless, he watched its silhouette. It noisily passed through the swamp. Crunchy the frozen ground and swamp grass as it made its way to safety. He was attempting to see if it was a buck or not, but it proved impossible. He looked to the East and sunlight began to creep over the horizon. 700,000 hunters across the Badger State were seeing this same sun rise, and it was the greatest feeling of anticipation and excitement these hunters would enjoy for another year to come.

The dawn of opening morning is like no other. The hope and excitement in the deer hunter is greater than any other time of the year. The light from the sun slices through the trees, casting shadows, and uncovering the woods. Slowly the woods come alive. Birds chirping, squirrels scampering, and already in the distance, a deer traveling through the swamp. It was out of range, but it was a good sign. The sunrise brought much anticipated warmth and visibility.

There had been several opening weekends where no one had tagged a deer. Good thing there was more to this weekend than just tagging a buck! This weekend would prove to be different, as that deer made its way slowly in the direction of Marlin who was hunting out of the Box Stand.

The deer disappeared into some swamp grass. The sound of footsteps crunching through the snow and frozen grass faded until they could no longer be heard. TJ could not see the animal anymore.

A few minutes later a shot rang out. Just one shot. A blaze orange blob moved through the swamp from the box stand. As TJ watched from 200 hundred yards away, he caught movement to his right. Other deer were moving near a tree line, and they saw Marlin move toward the deer he had just shot. The deer began jumping into the deep of the swamp, flashes of white followed and soon out of sight. TJ's heart began beating faster and adrenaline flowed through his veins. He had once thought that if that feeling ever failed to appear, he would know his hunting days were over. But after 25 years of the hunt, it was present as ever.

As Marlin continued to move toward the deer he just shot, TJ caught a glimpse of more movement. About 50 yards from where Marlin was, a large deer slipped into the swamp. The swamp was thick and dark at this time of the morning. Each of the hunters were using shotguns, as the law was for this part of the state. No scopes. Just iron sights.

The deer seemed to disappear. His heart racing a bit, TJ kept his eyes on the area he had last seen it, but it was gone. He turned his attention back toward Marlin. They had a standing rule. Tag it and wait. Especially on opening morning. This allowed the others to keep hunting, but you knew help would come to help you gut it and take it out of the woods.

So, TJ continued to hunt, as they all did. The sun was above the tips of the trees at this point. The air was still cold, and the sun was little relief. The steady west wind fell upon his face, but it was not too bad. At times, his eyes would water up, but that would be the only issue.

He kept scanning the swamp, minutes had passed, and he looked in the direction of Pete to the west, and he saw a statue of blaze orange 300 yards away. He wished him good luck in his thoughts. He swiveled his head back to the area in front of his stand, and when he stopped, a large buck was broadside moving through the swamp 75 yards away.

He could only think this was the buck that Uncle had seen, as he raised his gun, and attempted to get his iron sights on the buck. He was moving at a steady speed, and in an out of thick cover. Even from that distance, and through the swamp grass, TJ could see he was a big deer with quite a rack. The rack looked dark with high tines. This must be the one. His luck was changing.

And then...the buck was gone. TJ could not believe it! The buck disappeared just as he was getting ready to pull the trigger. He frantically looked for any movement where he last saw the buck. A minute or two had gone by, and then he saw movement 100 yards away. The buck crossed an opening on the outskirts of the swamp. TJ looked toward Pete who seemed to raise his gun, and then a shot rang out! *Did Pete get the monster buck*?! TJ stood and sat trying to get a view of the situation.

He saw the buck. It was running to the south and it was gone again. Pete made no attempt to shoot again, and he acted as if he clearly missed. Later, he would tell the store in which his slug hit a tree next to the big buck. The buck was on the property still, and he was as big as Uncle talked about it. This would prove to be an unforgettable hunt.

TJ slowly turned his attention back to the area in front of his wooden ladder stand. As he scanned the area for deer, he saw his brother-in-law back over by the area where his deer was shot. TJ, thought for a moment, and decided to help him out. He unloaded the chambered slug before descending, gave out a little sigh, and began to climb down the stand.

As he moved down the wooden ladder, it creaked a little, and there was a little wobbliness to it, but it had always been that way. The stand was a simple, wooden platform between to swamp oak trees, and one would ascend or descend from it using the wooden ladder.

As he touched down, his boot made a crunching sound as it met the snow.

TJ made his way through the swamp. Luckily the swamp was frozen over, and the walking was not too bad. His boots crunched here and there on the snow and dry swamp grass, and he continued to walk. Marlin was hunched over working on field-dressing the deer.

He approached Marlin and yelled out, "What did you get?!"

Marlin yelled back, "a doe."

TJ walked up on the doe which was lying dead on the ground. It was a good-sized deer, and you could see the pride coming off Marlin. Marlin was about half-way through cutting up the belly of the deer, careful not to get the stomach. TJ stayed and helped Marlin finish the job. They tied up the front legs to the head and started pulling the doe out of the edge of the swamp and toward the gravel road.

Chapter 5

A few hours later, Marlin, TJ, and Father were back at the shack, and had hoisted Marlin's deer up to the deer pole. They were talking inside the shack when Pete walked into the shack, slammed the door, and slung his hat to the floor. His boots and pants were all wet and muddy, and he looked terrible and mad.

He quickly took his parka off and put it on a hook on the door. He looked at all of them and let out a deep sigh. His pants were wet, and there was mud all over them as well. Everyone just looked at him, waiting for words to come out of his mouth. "I can't believe it." He said this multiple times, and then sat down at a chair at the table.

He began to slowly but surely tell his tale.

"I was on the edge of the swamp, taking a stand near a raggedy old tree. I was watching over an area that deer may be passing through. When all of a sudden, a doe seemed to pop up out of the swamp grass to my left.

"I brought my gun up quickly and the deer caught the movement, and began to leap away, so He fired off a slug, and then another, but I missed again!"

He was using an old 12-gauge gun he got from his father-in-law that he used for duck hunting. He missed, and the deer headed into the thick of the swamp.

The doe made a mistake and headed through a spot that had sometimes had deeper water in it. At the time, a layer of ice was covering it. Pete fired another shot and moved toward where he originally shot the deer. As he got closer to the swamp, as he took steps he broke through the thick layer of ice, and it went up to his knees.

Pete wasn't moving fast, but breathing heavy, but as he looked up the doe was in the same situation. It had broken through the ice as they'll, and somewhat stuck in the swamp water and mud. Between them were swamp grass and bushes. He couldn't get a clean shot. Sweating at this point, as he continued to make his way in and out of the swamp water, ice, and mud. He felt he was lifting each leg out of wet cement. But he continued forward.

The deer also continued and was making slow progress. It breathed heavily, and seemed exhausted, and came to a point where it just stood in the water and mud that reached up to its belly. Pete continued.

"I finally turned the corner around some thick brush, and I had a clear shot to the deer. We just stared at each other for a second, and I brought up my gun. 20 yards away. I was lining up the site with the deer, and I pulled the trigger...click."

The deer flinched, and mustered up its last bit of energy, and bounded out of the deep water and mud, and sprang then moved slowly to the security of the swamp."

"I just stood there. I couldn't believe it." Pete continued.

Well, Pete also duck hunted in the fall, and he was using his duck hunting shot gun. Duck hunters know what happened without being told...the shotgun plug was still in his gun. This device only allows a duck hunter to put three shells into his gun. Pete never removed it. Normally a shotgun holds 5 shells. When he aimed for the last time at the doe, he was expecting to use his fourth shell, but no more shells were in the gun. The doe looked at Pete and then found enough strength to bound away.

He sat down on one of the chairs and sighed deeply with a look of defeat written on his face. TJ offered him a hit from his flask, and he slowly took it, and took a deep snort, and his hunting for the day was over.

His companions reassured him that he still had next weekend, with that big buck out there as well. Pete stood up and resigned to his bunk. He did not always have the best luck while hunting. He was a heck of a fisherman, but more times than not, things didn't go his way during the hunt.

A blue-collar guy, who worked hard physical jobs most of his life. Married with kids, and probably the epitome of a Midwestern guy. He was always there for TJ through thick and thin. Hospital stays. The divorce. Help with his kids.

Pete laid in his bunk with most of his hunting clothing still damp and still on, and simply stared at the ceiling. He thought of past hunts that went awry, and how he waited for this weekend each year, and all he could think of was he blew it again. It's not like he hadn't gotten his share of deer, but they seemed to come few and far between.

As he continued to stare at the ceiling, his eyelids became tired and heavy. It didn't take long until the snoring commenced. He would get over the missed opportunity. He was a resilient guy. At 1:00 pm he was fast asleep exhausted. He didn't wake up until dinner.

Chapter 6

As they gathered Saturday evening in the shack after a long day of hunting, and with one deer on the buck pole, they settled into their normal Saturday night routine. There was a local registration station nearby, which conveniently also served as a tavern, and they would go there to register the deer. For the area, this was the place to be for part of the night especially if you had a deer to register, and even more so if you had a nice buck to show for your hunt.

They headed out. This place was a bit of a drive, but it was always a given they were going.

As they pulled in the parking lot, they saw that it was half-full, with mainly pick-up trucks. The sign of successful hunters were the trucks with the tailgates down. This was a sure sign of success for the day. If you were unlucky you walked around a little envious, but still happy for those hunters. Once they finished registering Marlin's deer out in the parking lot, they walked around a little bit more surveying the scene. They began walking toward the tavern, with its neon signs glowing from the windows welcoming the hunters to an oasis of warmth and beer.

They surveyed trucks and the deer sticking out of them, as they moved around the parking lot. They went inside and the tavern was filled with a lot of blaze orange. Blobs of it standing and moving around from one area to the next. Father made his way to the bar, sidestepping here and there a slightly staggering hunter. Eventually he made it to the bar, and he bought a pitcher of Miller Lite. There was hustle and bustle to the crowd.

Father enjoyed buying a pitcher of beer for his boys. It was not that often they were all together. The rest of them made their way to a tall table, and they soaked in the conversations near them.

Father bounced that pitcher of beer on the table almost spilling it, "You've been drinking already!" Pete said.

Father shot him a quick stern glance that turned into a smile.

The day was almost complete. It was great to be back at the tavern. There was a true rustic feeling to it, and a favorite of this group of hunters.

Across the other side of the bar was an old antler mount on the wall. It had always been there. It was a 10-point buck, but it was a heavy dark rack, with irregular points on the base of the antlers and it had a non-typical look to it. It always inspired thoughts of chasing a big buck in the woods and gave inspiration to the next day's hunt. On another wall was a wide set of bull horns set between some horseshoes mounted on the wall.

The bar bustled a bit, and Father poured each of his guys a beer. The cold, golden liquid smoothly ran out of that glass pitcher and into the glass pints, with a little foam floating at the top. They picked up and tipped their glasses to a good first day of the hunt. The bar was a mix of camo and blaze orange hats and parkas. Mostly men, but a handful of women as well. A slight fog of smoke clung to the rafters from the cigarettes and cigars.

"Not a huge crowd tonight," Marlin stated.

They all nodded in agreement. There were a lot of people in the bar that night, but there was a time when you couldn't even find a seat. It seemed every year the number of hunters was declining, and it could be seen just by walking in this bar.

"Anyone hear where Ol'Hutch is hunting this year?" asked Pete.

"I think he is up at some land north of here a bit. He usually comes back to hunt the farm next week and over Thanksgiving Weekend," stated TJ.

He tried to keep track of the grizzled hunters hunting patterns, as he was a family legend and his hunting mentor so to say. He was a war veteran, who lived his life by his own standards and not by anyone else's. He trapped, hunted, fished, and loved his family.

When TJ was younger, Ol'Hutch took him under his wing, as he showed him how to bow hunt, and then the tricks of gun hunting on the farm as well. He only lived a few miles away, but he gun-hunted elsewhere opening weekend. TJ was looking forward to seeing him later in the week.

Ol' Hutch knew the family property and the property around it like the back of his hand, and showed TJ the ins and outs, or at least told him about it, and TJ would always intently listen and watch the veteran hunter.

"That man knows this property so well it's scary," TJ stated with raised eyebrow.

They all nodded their heads in agreement, as it was no secret Ol' Hutch could hunt.

The men looked around the room, and noticed the crowd getting a little bigger and louder. They talked and drank beer for a little longer, but it didn't take long, and the beer was gone, and that brought about their exit. The group made their way through the smoke filled, crowded bar, and the crowd parted as they made their way to the door. This is not a place you tip toe through. You walked through with confidence and intent, and the four of them were an unintentional formidable pack.

They never stayed too long. While this was a favorite place, they wanted to get back to the shack. If one lingered too long trouble seemed to find its way into the tavern.

They left the tavern and that cold wind greeted them like it left them. A little sting to the face and they made their way to the truck. The heavy doors slammed, and from inside, their frozen breaths created a seemingly smoke-filled truck cab.

It was cold. The engine on that old truck revved up, and Father put it into gear. They made their way back to the shack, and as they turned into the drive two does were standing right there! Always a good sign! The truck came to a very noisy halt, and the deer scattered. The lights of the truck fell over part of the shack, and they were happy to be back. The night had just begun.

It was time to play some cards. They all sailed into the cabin, as much as a few two hundred pounders plus could sail that is. The coin bags found their way to the table. Marlin grabbed some beers, and TJ grabbed his flask. "Time for a little Bourbon, thank you very much," he said, declining the beer, and giving Marlin a sly wink.

The little table had just enough chairs for the four of them, and Pete started calling the game 5 card draw deuces are wild! In the background, on an old little black radio, that sat upon an old shelf, played Kenny Roger's *The Gambler.*

"Someone throw wood in the fire," Father demanded.

"Got it," TJ grabbed two logs and placed them into the wood burning stove.

They pulled out their coins and dollar bills and were ready to lose it all or win it all. It was all for fun and the pots rarely got too far out of hand. Except the time Marlin almost bet away all his gas money. He was sweating that game out for sure! After a run of bad luck, his luck changed and he won the pot, which was mostly his own money.

There almost never was any bad blood over poker at deer camp. The purpose was to have a little fun and feel lucky if the deer hunting gods permitted it.

The quarter ante from the players made its way to the middle of the table, with coins clinking together as they rolled into the pot. The cards began flying out of the dealer's hand. The nickels and dimes were bet and lost, maybe a dollar here or there, the beer was sucked back, and the whiskey sipped.

"So, no deer for you hey there TJ?" said Marlin with a little friendly smirk.

Pete chimed in, "Not the mighty hunter this opening day huh?" The others chuckled a bit, and TJ looked up at the others with a sly grin, and he began to dramatically look over the walls of the shack where several of his antler mounts were from past hunts. His gaze landed on the head mount with a large eight-point rack, which was on the far wall. He then lazily pointed his finger at it and looked at each of his hunting buddies right in the eyes.

They all rolled their eyes, and he smiled and threw down his cards and cheerily yelled, "Full House, you sons of bitches!"

He won that hand, but the confidence would fade.

They were all joking around and Father made a comment about drying out damp clothes from the days hunt, and TJ remembered a time when Father dried a wet pair of gloves a little too well.

First Father is knowledgeable in most things mechanical and can fix most anything, and seems to know everything, and is usually "right" when he declares something.

So, when he was wrong about something and TJ was right, he had never let him forget it. This went back to a hunt long ago, when one of their first hunts at the shack was a wet one. It rained the first two days off and on, and they were constantly trying to keep gloves, parkas, hats dry.

The shack was littered with clothing. They hung things up from every possible nail or post they could find. Father came in from the hunt a little frustrated, and he quickly removed his wet gloves, well at least as fast as one can remove very wet gloves, and he tossed them on top of the wood stove.

This seemed odd to TJ simply thinking "they will burn, won't they?" He was 17 and not very experienced in the world, but he thought something wasn't right. "Hey dad, won't those burn?"

In a slightly cranky and know it all voice he exclaimed "No, they will be fine!"

A minute later a strange smell arose in the shack, and it wasn't due to belching or farting.

Sure, enough those gloves were melting away atop of the wood stove!

"Your gloves are burning!" TJ said.

"Shoot!" he said and brushed them quickly off the top of the wood stove.

He never said he told you so, but at least once a year he reminded him of the time he tossed his gloves on the wood stove.

As TJ fumbled through the old hunting and fishing magazines in the crate, he noticed an old one from when he was very young. It was an *Outdoor Life* Magazine, and on the cover of it was a picture of an 8-point buck looking upon his back trail. Its rack profiled, and its brown coat was in focus while the background was blurred.

Getting these magazines in the mail each month were highlights of his youth. This was before these magazines became political and had more advertisements than articles, and they simply reported on hunting, fishing, and the great outdoors. He would read about strategies to tag the big one and look through the ads at the latest hunting and fishing equipment. At some point growing up, he realized it was just stuff to waste money on.

He had a reliable gun for deer hunting and kept his outdoor equipment simple, and he seemed to do quite well despite a lack of new technologies and stuff. He kept it simple, and simple seemed to work just fine.

Looking through that old magazine brought a little smile to TJ's face, and he continued to finish that magazine, and pick up several more from the past. While reading some of them, he occasionally remembered an article or ad from the past, and that pleased him even more.

As the wood stove burned down, and the yawning at the table began, they called the last hand. It was pushing 10:30 pm, and they would be up early tomorrow. One by one they left the table in the middle of the shack, steel chairs scratching against the cement floor, as they were pushed in or aside.

Inside each man put aside his gear for the following morning, trying to pay attention to detail, but more concerned with getting to the bunks was on everyone's mind.

TJ stepped outside one last time, and the cold overcame him, but with whiskey running through him, he didn't notice too much. Pete was out there on his way back from the outhouse since Marlin was camped out in the shack bathroom. You could hear his boots heavily crunching through the snow. As he made his way out of the shadows, and into the light of the moon they greeted each other.

"Cold night," Pete said

"Not too bad though," replied TJ

"We've had colder," he added with little emotion.

They both stopped near each other and looked at the stars above. Frozen breaths rhythmically leaving their mouths as they stared at the night sky, a cold November breeze hitting their faces.

"How's home life these days?" Pete added. He knew the divorce had been hard on everyone.

Never looking at each other during the conversation. TJ sighed and slowly took out a slender, silver object. Unscrewed the top, and had a hit of whiskey. He then screwed the top back on.

"Things are good with the kids when I see them." TJ replied.

"How about you and her?" Pete glanced over but TJ only looked up at the stars and let out a little sigh.

He unscrewed the flask again and took a deeper sip. The whiskey burned as it ran down his throat. The metallic sound was clear as he screwed the cap back onto the flask.

He cringed slightly. He was almost numb to the cold at this point. The only sound was the wind moving through the trees. And the only motion was the frozen air filtering out of their mouths.

Pete with a helpless look on his face looked out to the dark woods, and he patted him on the shoulder and made his way back into the shack. Pete wanted to help but knew only time would heal things.

TJ stayed out a little longer...looked up at the moon and the stars. His head was a little dizzy from the whiskey he'd been drinking all night. He swayed slowly back and forth as he continued to stare into the night sky. The stars were quite bright tonight with the sky so clear. The snow had tapered off hours ago. He marveled at the moon and stars for a moment and walked back in the shack. The heavy shack door closed with a "thud" for the last time that night.

Chapter 7

Sunday morning came with the alarm clock ringing and breaking an almost silent shack.

The wood stove barely had a spark. The men moved a little slower this morning. Drinking and card playing most of the night seemed to extend their deep repose.

Nonetheless, similar routines once again began.

"Put wood in the stove!" Father yelled, from the comfort of his bunk. As the patriarch, he was the only one who could give this order, and someone else had to follow it. Pete was still snoring, and Marlin was tossing in his bed, but not ready to get out.

TJ was ready to go hunting and got himself moving by getting up and putting two logs in the dying wood stove. The metal handle of the stove was cold. Unlike the heat it contained the night before when it was running hot. He threw the wood in and latched the handle on the lock, the metal grated slightly as it hit other metal. And with a little grunting and groaning, he pushed off his knee and made his way to the coffee pot. He realized he did not attend to the coffee maker the night before, and apparently no one else had either. The morning routine was now in true motion.

Sunday morning at this deer camp is different than opening morning. For over 20 years, a tradition had been followed, and this Sunday would be no different. The group would have their coffee and be on stand at first light, but around nine o'clock am they came together for a hearty sit-down breakfast.

So, as the hunters filed out of the shack that morning, they knew they would be back in a few hours to warm up and eat a hot, hearty breakfast. A truly great Sunday morning for one of these hunters would be to have their deer down before Sunday breakfast. It happened probably every other year by at least one of them. It brought excitement and a brand-new story to tell at the breakfast table.

That would not be the case this Sunday morning. The hunt proved uneventful for some reason, and outside of seeing some deer in the distance not one of the hunters fired his gun. The cold was still hanging on, so the hunters were moving back toward the shack around 9:30 am. They each had approximately a half mile walk at least. TJ had the longest walk. His stand was about a mile.

Pete was the breakfast cook most of the time for the Sunday morning breakfast. He went in a little early to get things started. When he got in the shack father was already there placing logs in the woodstove.

As Marlin and TJ approached the shack, after meeting up out in the field, they noticed the smoke pouring out of the chimney. It was a welcome sight. They knew in a few minutes they would be walking into a warm, cozy shack. Marlin turned the handle on the door and a slight wave of warm wafted over them as they walked. The fire was producing some heat, but it was not fully roaring yet.

Pete was at the propane-powered stove, working over some scrambled eggs, and a skillet with sausage and bacon sizzling and popping in the hot grease. The aroma and sight was most welcoming to the cold hunters as they entered the shack. Sighs of relief came out from the two, and they stood in the warmth for a moment before they removed the winter gear.

"Coffee is ready if you want some," said Pete.

Father was reading an old hunting magazine, as he sat in grandpa's chair. Many of these were kept in the shack for down time reading. Outdoor Life, Field and Stream, and some books about adventures. He flipped through the pages.

"See anything?" came from behind the magazine. Marlin had seen some, but they were too far away to shoot. TJ simply said "Not much." He could sense the bad luck creeping up on him, but the morning breakfast would raise his spirits. The smell of cooking bacon and sausage filled the shack, along with frying eggs, and corned beef hash.

The coffee started pouring and the hunters began to thaw out from the morning hunt. Parkas began to shed, and the woodstove was truly doing its job. It had rekindled its life and once again the shack was a cozy wooden box.

"Breakfast is ready!" said Pete.

Movement began toward the table.

"Need help with anything?" Marlin asked.

"Nope take a seat," Pete said.

Mounds of scrambled eggs, and sizzling sausage, made its way onto the awaiting plates scattered on the table. Bacon was added for good measure. The steam from the food could be seen rising and disappearing into the height of the shack, and as it disappeared into the rafters TJ found his way to the table.

Many thanks were said, and the group began to eat. The other hunters were very much thankful and agreed as usual to clean up the breakfast mess. With full bellies and a warm shack everyone lingered longer than normal. Grandpa's chair was the coveted place to sit after such a breakfast. Everyone let Father get there first, and the rests found themselves at the table or washing dishes. The coffee continued to flow, and some discussion about where each would hunt as they would soon return to the woods. It was 11 am.

As TJ walked in from his stand and cut through the swamp instead of taking the longer way around. He also had the opportunity to jump a deer and move it toward Marlin. It was so cold that most of the water in the swamp had turned to ice, and this is the only time of the year it was easy to walk through the swamp. This would be a methodic walk. He would use what he learned from Ol' Hutch.

He would cut a deer trail and walk it. Venturing off to one side or another to push a thick patch of brush or willows. TJ got to a spot where an old stand was hung. It was in rough shape at this point, but it reminded him of a hunt from years past. He looked up at it with admiration, and with a reminiscing sentiment. He looked around the area and began thinking of past hunts. At one time, this was a honey-hole stand.

That year he had placed this stand here because he knew deer passed through this area as it was an escape route from an adjacent property. He would hunt it today.

It was mid-day and the deer were doing just what He thought they would do. For once at least. The pressure to get a deer slowly building, as opening weekend was usually the best chance to get a deer. He scanned the swamp for movement, but there wasn't any. He watched the birds fly by, and he felt the cold breeze on his cheek.

After an hour or so, He heard a shot ring out from an adjacent property. He held his gun tighter, and watched for movement from the direction of the shot. Five minutes later two deer approached. They were a hundred yards away, but they we're heading for the security of the swamp. He knew an opportunity would be coming. He discerned they were a doe and a small buck. Their heads bobbing and weaving through the swamp grass. Looked like a small 6-point buck.

They were alert with their eyes scanning and their ears moving like small radars. At 40 yards, he aimed at the one trailing the other. They were both average-sized. Even so as usual his heart raced a bit as it did. He put the sight low on the chest as it stood broadside to me. He waited until the buck stood still to check its back trail, and he squeezed the trigger. He hit it! He could see the hair explode from the body. He kept an eye on the doe as it ran. He expected it to stop. It never did.

Confusion and bewilderment came over him. He climbed down from the stand and quickly went over to where it stood before He shot. Deer hair was everywhere but He could not see any blood. The confusion continued.

He followed the trail the doe used as it lit out of the area, and He found no blood at all. He went back to the tree-stand a little disheartened, but He knew there were seven days left to hunt. He climbed the wooden ladder, and he continued his vigil.

A few hours later, the sun began to sink, and the shadows began to stretch. Deer movement generally happened at this time of the day as a natural part of the deer movement, but the last two days were anything but natural for the deer. Hunters had entered the woods, and that would greatly affect deer movement as well. He scanned the swamp with my eyes, and in his head He thought they would have about 15 more minutes of shooting light. Right then a shot rang out from the west. It must have been Pete hunting a tree-line behind the swamp.

He sat tight a little longer to see if anything would come his way, but then quickly but cautiously made my way down the ladder stand and toward my Pete. He cut followed a deer trail through the swamp that would lead me to the area my Pete was hunting. As he made his way over, he could see he was standing over a deer. The hunt was a success! He was happy for him as it had been a few years since he shot a deer with his gun. He quickly saw it was a buck of average size, and Pete was smiling.

He congratulated him and he took a closer look at the downed animal. There was a strange marking under its chest.

"What did you get?" TJ said.

"A little buck," Pete said.

49

"Nice shootin," said TJ.

TJ got closer to the spot where the deer was lying dead. He looked closer. It was missing a sizable patch of hair and skin from its underside, and the flesh was showing and newly scarred...he thought for a moment.

It was the buck he missed just hours ago! He could not believe it, and, so he had to share his story with Pete, and it brought wonder to him as well. They laughed for a moment. Pete told him how some deer had come out of the woods behind him. And then began to field- dress the deer together. That was the day they both shot the same deer.

When they got back to the shack, Pete showed the deer to Father and Marlin. They hung it up on the deer pole where it would hang until my father took it to be processed. It was Sunday night and the opening weekend was over. They had two deer to show for it. Marlin and Pete would begin their trek back to the big city, and TJ would stay on for the rest of the week, as he had planned that out.

He had never taken the whole week off before to stay and hunt, but he wanted to do it. With a few good-byes and closing doors deer camp was down to two hunters.

Chapter 8

The Monday after opening weekend is usually very different than the two days that just ended. Everything is quiet. You only hear an occasional shot, and it seems to echo forever as there are so few shots being fired. The only problem is the deer are not moving as much, as there are fewer hunters to move them around. No matter. TJ would enjoy having the entire property to himself. Uncle was gone visiting his daughters this week.

The weather improved and the sun was out. It must have reached 20 degrees. TJ would change his tactics today considering the deer would not be moving much after the onslaught of hunters and shooting in the woods yesterday. He left the shack a little after sun-up, and he began a walk that would take him throughout the entire property. He was looking forward to this.

After walking through the swamp, he rounded a willow thicket on the outskirts of the swamp, and began walking through a field of high grass, beaten down by the Wisconsin weather. As he took a few steps into the grass, a buck sprang from its bed 70 yards away, and began running, quartering away from the hunter.

The shotgun was instinctually shouldered and on the buck. The buck was about 70 yards away when it jumped up, and only a few yards further as the iron sights fell upon the body, and a blast from the shotgun threw the 1 oz slug through the air, and toward the deer.

The buck did not flinch it seemed, and it bounded on toward the swamp, and TJ let off two more slugs as it ran away, and seemingly they missed the mark.

It was an 8-point buck, but it seemed he had clearly missed. He stood for a moment, and continued to watch the buck run away, and then it was gone. He went over in his head what just happened. He felt like he missed, but he went to the spot he had first seen it just to check. Not checking to see if he wounded the animal would be shameful.

He made his way to the spot, and he looked around. He took a couple of steps toward the way the deer had exited the bed. Blood.

Blood was all over the place. He hit it with the first shot! From what he was seeing, the blood seemed to be spraying out of the buck as it bounded away. The trail was easy to follow, but he stopped about 20 yards into the blood trailing.

He had remembered a buck Marlin had shot years ago, and the blood trail was good, but they followed too quickly, and the buck was never found. This was on TJ's mind that morning.

So, he stopped and enjoyed the moment, and looked over the blood itself. It was no gut shot, there was bright red blood sprayed on the snow and the brush alongside the trail.

He thought for a moment. *There was not really a reason to wait with such a good blood trail.* But, he waited 15 minutes or so. He smiled as he waited, but he knew he couldn't simply count on it being dead already. So, after waiting a while, perhaps he should have waited longer, he began following the blood trail. With every step he took there was blood spray along the trail, but it continued to zig zag through the high grass and then near a tree-line, and then into the swamp. He halted. He looked back. He had covered at least 50 yards, but no deer yet. He was a little puzzled, but he knew a wounded deer could still travel far. But he thought. *There is so much blood.*

He hesitantly continued, and with each step expecting to see the body of a dead deer on the ground. The buck made its way near Uncle's Farmhouse. Still bleeding and leaving a good trail.

TJ grew concerned. The buck had travelled a hundred yards at this point, and it was still going. He stopped his search and backed off the trail after marking where he saw blood last. He had to give this deer time. A cold November wind hit the left side of his face as it blew from the north east. The weather was changing. He made a long walk back to the shack, with little hope of finding the deer.

He did make it back later in the morning, but the blood trail fizzled and led into a prairie of long grass. TJ looked around and a feeling of dread came over him like he never felt before. He stared into the prairie. His heart sank, and his stomach turned. He stood out in that vast prairie, wind smacking him in the face. He had never lost a deer before that he had hit. He was on his hands and knees scouring the ground for blood. *There's no blood.*

He didn't know what to do. The feeling of dread had turned physical. He could feel it through his whole body. He simply stared blankly into the 100-

acre prairie. He dropped to one knee, lost for words and action. He could only remember once feeling this way.

He was devastated. He would go back to look for the buck later in the day and days after, but to no avail. He had lost it. TJ made the long walk back to the shack.

He crossed the small road that was the last road to deer camp, and he walked through a field behind the shack.

He approached the shack but today was different. Today no warm fire would be greeting him no smoke was pouring out of the chimney. Today he was alone. Pete and Marlin left late Sunday evening, to return home to their families. Father had returned home to Mother. He would return during the week, but TJ was alone.

He opened the door to the shack, and the stillness and quietness felt awkward. But that moment was fleeting, as a peacefulness came over him. He was gone for a good part of the day, so the air was stiff and the Shack was cold since the fire went out hours ago. The coldness was still and heavy. Unwelcoming.

He removed his gloves and took his parka off and left them on the small couch next to the wall. He walked over to the wood stove and grabbed the steel handle and opened it. He turned it and opened the door to feed the stove. He laid in some crumpled up old sheets of newspaper. He reached for some small kindling in the wood bin, and he started laying it in the stove. TJ then reached for the box of matches.

He struck the match alongside the box creating the slight grating sound that is also familiar to those who make fires. The small flame quickly lit up the match. He slightly angled it down and into the stove, and let it burn down the stick for a moment. He moved the match slowly towards the fire and then slowly to the paper. He moved the burning match to the other side of the stove and let another piece of paper and quickly the flame spread towards the wood through the paper in the fire.

He shut the door, and turned the metal handle, locking the door. A quiet grating sound filled the shack. He stood by the stove for a moment. As he stood, he looked up and stared through the window. Darkness was setting on the shack, and he turned on the small light next to grandpa's chair. He glanced around the shack and realized he was hungry.

That night he had more chili for dinner. After warming it up on the stove, he scooped some into a bowl. He set the bowl down and grabbed a spoon. The chili was steaming hot, and as he added some shredded cheese, it melted quickly.

He had been looking forward to this meal all day, and he was glad to be sitting at the table with warm food to eat. Yet, it was odd to be alone at the table. The only sounds were the popping and crackling of the woodstove. Only nights before the shack had an abuzz about the place, and it felt like deer camp.

Yet, there was something to be said for solitude. It gave him time to look around the shack, be at one with these thoughts, and reminisce of past hunts and vacations at the shack. He began to feel differently.

He stopped thinking about the lost buck for a moment, and he tried to think of something else.

A smile crept over his face; a sense of peace again set within him. He glanced to the walls, and his eyes rolled over several of the antler mounts. As he looked at them, he remembered past hunts, past successes and failures, but were all good memories. After all, one should learn from failures, and he tried to.

He finished his chili and headed over to the counter and had a glass of water, then cleaned up his bowl and dinner. A proud and accomplished sigh came from him as he knew is now time to relax. He walked over to a small bookshelf that seemed to be at the shack forever, but he could not right remember when it got there. Books from the past that were remnants of rummage sales and old purchases, gifts and such.

He looked over the titles of the books by Hemingway, MacClean, O'Conner, Thoreau, and McManus. His eyes continued to scan the titles, and his fingers were gliding over the binding edge of each. He continued pass the classics then stopped at a very special book if he remembered correctly an old rummage sale purchase from his childhood by his mother. A Compilation of Outdoor Life stories from Outdoor Life magazine.

At the age of 10, he began reading through this book and it truly ignited his sense of adventure. This was his favorite book to read while at deer camp no question. He slid the book out from the bookshelf. The smooth leather like cover was now in his hands, and he looked it over and smiled.

He made his way over to grandpa's old chair where the reading light was nearby, and it was already on. He set the book down on the chair and walked over to a small counter near an old cast iron sink. he grabbed the neck of a bottle of bourbon, and a glass. He began to pour it halfway full.

He enjoyed the whiskey, but it also serves him later in the night when eventually as always, the bad thoughts came. He slowly made his way back to grandpa's chair. He set the small glass of whiskey down on a small crate, and slowly sat down in the chair. The chair was a welcome feeling. Not too hard, and not too soft. The material was scratchy rather than smooth, and at the end of the arm of the chair were wooden endings. This chair was truly vintage.

With the book in his lap, he began to flip through the pages. There were probably 60 stories in this collection.

He came upon the story about the Jordan Buck. If you hunt in Wisconsin, and you don't know that story, you should read about it. In his mind, he soaked up each detail of the hunt as it was written. He sat there and put himself in Jordan's boots, following those giant tracks through the snow near Danbury, WI.

Simultaneously, TJ slowly reached for his whiskey. Took a small sip and continued reading. The light from the small lamp cut half of him in the shadows with the light radiating over the book. A small glow from the old wood stove as he sat in the half light of the shack, and he closed the book as he finished the story. He looked at his empty glass. He looked up and around the shack which was mostly in the dark. The antler mounts on the wall could barely be seen.

As a shack grew darker so did his thoughts. His thoughts focused on his personal failures mainly his failed marriage.

He got up from the chair and made his way to the small counter next to an old sink. He grabbed the bottle and poured himself another glass of the whiskey.

His heart grew cold, and despair set in, as he looked out the window over the cast- iron sink. He could see the outline of some trees in the woods, but with a closer glance he could see a slight reflection of himself in the window. He turned away with whisky in hand and a grimace on his face.

He made his way back to the chair. Memories from the past, fear of the future, events created in his mind that had not even happened. Beads of sweat started to dot his forehead.

Things just didn't work out. He was sorry for how things turned out, and how he treated her. There was regret. He slowly got up from the chair a little unsteady at this point to make his way to the counter for another glass. This would not be his last trip to the counter. Eventually he stumbled his way to his bunk forgetting to turn off the little light. It continued to illuminate a soft glow in the room, next to the empty chair, with the book laying sloppily upon it.

Chapter 9

It was about noon, when TJ headed toward the Creek Bottom. He had hunted the morning to no avail. He was in a cut corn field, walking the edge of it, as he made his way toward the creek bottom. At times, he would step on a corn stalk and it would crackle a little as he shifted his weight, but otherwise he kept his walk quiet. He had decided to hunt his old ladder stand on the other side of the creek, on the edge of Maggie's property.

He left the corn field and dropped down toward the creek. He made his way as quietly as he could, and the snow seemed to be a little powdery, which helped. He had a small feeling of hope with this idea to hunt the creek bottom, but he would have to cross the tree bridge in order to get to his stand.

An old massive oak had fallen from one side of the creek to the other many years ago. None of the hunters knew exactly when. It just always seemed to be there. The trunk was so huge you could walk over it with confidence...most of the time. The only time it was questionable was when the weather turned bad, which is exactly the situation TJ found himself in.

He got to the Tree Bridge and looked down to the other side, and it looked like three inches of snow covered it. The old oak fell from one side of the bank to the other, probably in a big storm. TJ grimaced. There was also a little wind swirling down in the creek bottom, and he realized this may not be a simple walk in the woods. One slip and you fell into the icy creek below that at this time of the year could be about 8 feet deep, and the old oak happened to be right over one of the deeper parts of the creek.

Pete may have fallen in once and just never told anyone. That could have happened. But TJ had never fallen in.

As he stood on the bank, he looked at the water below, and it was moving quickly under the old oak. TJ grabbed a hefty stick and used it to steady himself as he moved onto the trunk of the oak. He then dropped the stick to the ground. It fell with a slight "thud." *Should have held on to it to help me across.*

With his Winchester cradled in his arms in front of him, in order to balance everything out, and a small pack around his waist, he began to take a step toward the other side of the bank. The first few steps he moved with hesitancy, and as he took the fourth, he wobbled, but caught his balance. He took a deep breath and realized he just needed to do it.

Cautiously but with a little haste, he moved over the trunk and toward the bank. With each step snow spilled over and onto the moving creek. TJ looked down. The tree was about a foot over the moving water. TJ got a little dizzy looking down, and quickly looked back up and took a step at the same time. He was approaching the end of the tree-bridge, but as he looked up, he was staring directly at a buck.

It was the buck. The one Uncle had seen Friday night near the farmhouse. It had to be. The rack was dark, massive and the buck itself was huge. They both stared at each other. TJ was off balance with one foot ahead of the other and out in front of him. He began to shake a bit. He knew this may be a once in a lifetime chance to get this huge buck. *I'll pull my gun up quickly and see if I can fire off a shot.*

The buck just stood there, 30 yards away. Daring him.

In one swift motion, TJ swung his gun from its cradled position, and was bringing it up to a shooting position when it happened... his foot slipped when he shifted the gun, and with a loud gasp he tumbled into the icy creek below. As he fell the shotgun left his hand and flew toward the bank behind him.

With a winter parka on, and a heavy pair of boots, he went right to the bottom in a splash that could have been heard far away, but no one was there to hear it.

There was simply silence, and the big buck bounded off.

Under the water, with a current pushing him, he opened his eyes to a dark reality. He was frightened for a moment, but then he pushed off the bottom and sprung to the top. He reached the top of the water and gasped for air. And attempted swimming, but with all the clothing on it was more of a desperate doggy paddle.

He tried to head to the bank. The banks of this creek were all high, and pulling oneself out would not be easy.

Then, all a sudden, he disappeared under the water, and all was quiet again. The woods were oddly still. Until a bird chirped on a branch nearby.

Suddenly, an out-stretched hand came out of the water, broke through a sheet of thin ice on the bank, and he clung to the edge of the bank. TJ reappeared and his fingers dug into the hard soil on the creek bank. He now clung with both hands and gasped for air several times. He laid there, outstretched for a moment, most of his body still in the water. He took another deep breath and looked around. Looking for a part of the bank that was not so steep. Nothing was to be found. The damp cold smell of the soil in the bank resonated through his nostrils.

He looked around and noticed a thick root protruding from the bank and it climbed up toward the top of the bank. He would have to pull himself up. The cold was truly setting in. His mustache and beard were covered with ice, especially around his mouth. He grabbed the root and began to pull, and at the same time he was kicking and clawing with his boots. He was slowly pulling himself out of the water. Clawing his way up the steep bank he finally made it to the top of the bank and with the last of his energy rolled up and over to the flat ground. Exhaustion overcame him as he laid there, but he was now worried about hypothermia. He began shaking badly.

He knew he had to get up and move around. He peeled off the soaking wet parka and let it fall to the ground. He then fell to his hands and knees. He looked around, and he knew one would be around to help. The wind was picking up. It was a mile walk back to the shack. His hands were in about two inches of snow when he realized again, he was freezing. He had to move now. There was no help coming.

Hypothermia. He pushed himself up to a standing position, and with his arms crossed in front of him, and his hands under his armpits, he began walking.

He made his way up and out of the creek bottom, and he fell to his knees again as he hit the cut corn field.

He couldn't feel his toes. His boots felt like blocks of ice, but he decided to keep them on. He got up and began walking again. He leaned slightly into the wind and again had his arms crossed in front of him. He only had a wet flannel and wool sweater on top and his soaked long underwear beneath a pair of hunting pants. He reached the edge of the corn field and decided to take a shortcut that would bring him behind the shack. He would have to cut through another large cut corn field and then through a small woodlot.

He fell to his knees as he looked over the last corn field he needed to cross, and he brought his cold fingers up to his mouth. He began blowing warm air onto them for a minute or so and then stuffed them back under his armpits.

As he crossed the open corn field, he felt the full effect of the cold November wind, cutting him with each step he took. He knew if he reached the wood lot it would offer shelter from some of that wind. Halfway across the field he felt himself trembling nonstop, and he was exhausted. He could not feel his feet anymore, and he stumbled to the cold, icy ground. His hands were still tucked under him as he fell, so his shoulder went down first and then his face. The snow and ice cut his face, and from a small cut, blood began to stream. He got to his knees and looked down and saw speckles of red in the snow below him. He reached and felt his face with his cold hands. He could barely feel anything. He thought about his kids for a moment.

He looked around, hoping to see another hunter, but given it was a Tuesday, there was no one else around. He sat there on his knees, eyes watering, and his body shutting down, he slowly got to his feet. Still shaking and trembling from the wet and cold, he made it to the woodlot and stood and took a moment to survey where he was. He headed toward where he thought the shack would be. He stumbled through the woodlot, tripping on unseen dead branches, and getting caught in bramble. He was losing his wits and his strength was all but gone. He weaved through the woodlot.

The shack door slammed open, and TJ poured himself into the shelter. He made it back. There was still some warmth in the shack as the fire had not died out yet. He crawled on the cold cement floor until he came to an old rug, and when he reached it, he collapsed on it, near the fire.

That evening he was sitting in grandpa's old chair wrapped in a gray, wool blanket and eating chili. He eventually thawed out, and he avoided hyperthermia. The crackling of the old radio resonated softly throughout the shack. He sat and ate his dinner slowly, and he drank some water from a small glass cup.

At that time, he realized his shotgun was at the edge of the creek, and that his parka was down there too. The crazy son of a bitch was still thinking about hunting. He may have to take some time off the next day, but in his head, he knew he would be back out. He had been face to face with the big buck.

He finished his venison chili, dropped it off at the sink, and headed to his bunk. In his fresh pair of long underwear and a flannel, he slowly crawled into his sleeping bag. Moments later he was fast asleep. The only sounds he heard in the shack was the crackling of the fire, and the ticking of a clock.

Chapter 10

He woke the next morning, still tired from his ordeal. He was thirsty. His mouth was dry. The shack was cold. The fire had not been kept up. He swung his feet from the bed to the cold floor. It made him flinch.

He got up with a shiver, and he made his way to the sink. He turned the old metal sink handle and placed his cup underneath and he filled it half full. Cold water ran over his lips and his thirst felt quenched.

He stared out the window above the sink to the back of the shack. The wood-line was about 20 yards away. Between it was a space where the old hand pump had once stood. As a child, he and his brother pumped water for the family during vacations.

It was faded red, just like the shack, even when he was a child. It stood about 4 feet off the ground. On the side of the hand pump was an old tin ladle. After they had primed and pumped water into a water cooler that would sit in the shack, they would take a drink for themselves.

He remembered his brother would pump while he filled the tin ladle. The water would rush out fast, and splash into the ladle. The sunshine glimmered like diamonds in the water. He brought the ladle up to his mouth slightly leaning into it. The water was cold and wonderful. As he poured it into his mouth, half of it ran down his chin.

A smile came over his face, as TJ stared out the window upon the past. He drank the rest of the glass and made his way back to the bunk. In a few minutes he was sleeping again. He would not hunt that day.

Wednesday morning he sat near the wood stove with a small glass of coffee beside him on the table. The wood stove cracked and popped and radiated heat.

He would not be hunting that morning, as he was recovering. Thoughts came back to the hunt. He sat in grandpa's chair slowly rocking and sipping the coffee when he wondered if he would see an Ol' Hutch out in the woods this week. Ol' Hutch was a term of endearment.

Once TJ was hunting from the swamp stand years ago, and it was around 7:00 am. Plenty of time after first light, and he caught movement to his left, and he saw a hunter in dull, blaze orange standing on a tree-line a couple of hundred yards away. He knew it was Old Hutch simply by his appearance and silhouette. He always seemed to stand tall and was a lean man. These features were easy to see even from quite a distance.

He was "still hunting." Walk. Look. Wait. Walk... Look... Wait. Work the cover and jump a deer. Shoot while it's running or wait for it to possibly stop. This was artwork.

TJ watched from his stand as he continued. He was walking through some brush. *Slowly.* He would take five steps or so and stop, in and out of cover quietly, but not too quiet. He was circling TJ's position as he knew he was there as blaze orange sticks out a long way. He knew he may push a deer toward TJ, and he would have been as equally happy as shooting one himself. He began to work his way through the swamp and in TJ's direction. He circled around and that is when two deer jumped up and ran farther into the swamp. He raised his gun, but he did not shoot.

He waited. While one of the deer continued to run and bound through the swamp. One stopped, as at times whitetails will do to check what the danger was. The small buck stopped and looked back. Ol'Hutch counted on that. A single shot rang out through the swamp. That was the last mistake that deer would make. It was like watching an artist create a masterpiece.

TJ remembered asking Old Hutch one time why he wasn't on stand at first light and why he didn't start hunting until past sun-up. He simply said "You can't shoot what you can't see." He would think often on those words.

As the morning continued, TJ was still in Grandpa's chair, drinking coffee. He looked around the cabin and saw the antlers of the first buck he ever shot with a gun, mounted on the wall. It was just a small fork-horn, but it always made him smile.

As he thought about that hunt, he could see it all again. He was in his Swamp Stand on a Sunday morning. Father was walking the swamp's eastern edge, and two deer watched for a moment, and then quickly bounded away into the swamp. Adrenaline ran through his body, but he stayed calm. The doe was in front, and a buck trailed behind. Each bounding through the swamp grass looking to reach the safety of the swamp. His stand was just inside the thick cover, and he readied his gun as they covered the ground quickly. He could see the breath pour out of their mouths, and their muscles tensed with every move. They were on a trail that zig-zagged through the swamp grass, and He was relatively close to the trial TJ was covering from above.

The Swamp Stand was made years ago by TJ but with help from one of his uncles. It was originally for bow hunting, but it proved to be a better stand for gun hunting. It was a handful of 2x4's and a sheet of plywood along with a ladder they made. It was placed between two Scrub Oak trees. He and other relatives have taken quite a few deer from this stand. Each deer hunting property has a honey-hole stand like this one. It overlooked a few deer trails that led in and out of the swamp.

As the buck and doe came closer, he hovered above as the deer took one of the trails into the swamp. It was a trail that would have them broadside to him at about 40 yards. They continued to bound, making it challenging to stay on them with the gun. The buck followed the doe, and they were getting close to the thick cover and now were broadside at 30 yards.

He put the sight on the buck, and he followed it as it bounded and at its highest point, He pulled the trigger on the old Winchester. A cloud of smoke, and loud "bang" broke the silence. He only saw the doe bound away. He scanned the swamp grass for movement from the deer. He believed he dropped it on the spot. Adrenaline flowed over him as well as excitement and anticipation. He calmed down and pulled himself together. He was shaking a bit as He climbed down that wobbly wooden ladder.

When he got to the ground it was hard to pinpoint where he shot the deer. He made his way in the direction, but he had not seen anything. *Did it move away hidden in the swamp grass?!* A slight wave of concern came over him, but he continued at a faster pace.

He was stepping quickly over bent swamp grass, and Knowles, tripping a bit. His boots crunched the hard snow. He could only hear himself breathing and the crunching of the snow. He got to the area and looked around anxiously, and the buck was right where he shot it. TJ simply lost track of that areas as he got down from this stand. It was his first buck.

Later that morning, TJ found himself walking back down to the creek bottom to retrieve his blaze orange parka and his shotgun. He was approaching the area of the tree bridge and he slowed down, and he looked around. He then continued walking until he saw his parka, and he looked toward the creek bank and he could see the top of his shotgun barrel pointed toward the sky. TJ looked over the tree bridge and beyond, where the big buck stood less than 48 hours ago. He grabbed the parka it was frozen and hard, and TJ thought back upon his almost near-death experience. At least he felt that way at the time. He picked up the parka and went to the creek bank, and then he went to pick up his shotgun while dropping the parka at the same time.

He pulled the shotgun from the icy edge of the creek bed, and he wiped it off with the sleeve of his jacket he had on. He engaged the action of the shotgun, and with a few slides of the action, all seemed fine. He knew he would have to go back to the shack and give it a thorough cleaning though.

He picked up the parka again, and with the shotgun in the other hand he made his way out of the creek bed and toward the shack. He kept thinking of the missed opportunity with the big buck and the negative thoughts began all over again.

Wednesday afternoon found TJ back at the Tavern, but alone.

At the bar, he sat there, three whiskeys in, glassy eyed and tearing up the cocktail napkin. He looked into his drink and stared intently. Looking for something that he couldn't find. The bar was empty. Hank Williams Jr. sang *Whiskey Bent and Hell Bound.*

The bartender was on a stool, about 10 feet away, watching the TV and smoking a cigarette. Luckily neither of them wanted conversation, and neither were going to get it from the other.

TJ looked up from his drink, and looked around the bar. Still, no one was there. He made a big sigh, and he went back to looking for answers toward the bottom of his glass of whiskey. Maybe if he finished it quickly, the answers would be there. They never were.

As he took another sip, three men walked in the Tavern. One had a Bears hat. FIBS...he thought to himself. They must have been hunters. They were dressed in some newly purchased camo, and blaze orange it seemed. He looked them over as they sat down and went back to minding his business.

Unfortunately, those fellas were not going to be minding theirs. They ordered beer and began talking loudly about hunting and fishing. They evidently had already started drinking prior to their arrival at the tavern. TJ listened for a minute, and quickly felt they were full of shit, and looked up at the TV.

Then from across the bar, one of the men shouted to him.

"Tough day!?"

TJ looked up and gave them the slightest nod. The men were snickering quietly to one another.

They laughed and one whispered loudly.

"I'd drink like that too, if I had no friends."

TJ looked about and realized he had lingered too long at the tavern. Never one to look for trouble...most of the time. He just stared at them for a few seconds and then looked back at the TV.

A peanut shell went across the bar, and just missed TJ. He looked up again, and without hesitation, got up and walked around the horseshoe-shaped bar.

He went up to the first guy, and he asked what his problem was.

The guy was not quite so brave now. His friend chimed in,

"You're the problem."

He then realized this was not going to go well. TJ looked back over to the first guy and when he did. He caught the motion of the second man, and his fist hit TJ in the side of the face.

TJ stumbled back a few feet, and then he lunged at the second man and took him to the ground, and in full guard and punched him in the face. Blood sprang from the man's nose, and then from behind TJ felt a punch to his back. TJ fell over to the ground, and he managed to get up to face the two men still standing.

Then the bartender was over and managed to separate the men. The bartender kicked the three out of the bar, and it was over. TJ shook his head to gain his wits, and felt blood on his lip, and wiped it off. A red mark left on his cheek.

He stumbled back over to the bar, but picked up his hat first, and he quickly slammed the rest of his whiskey. Then glared at the men as they left the bar. He then looked down at the bottom of his glass. Again, there were no answers.

Chapter 11

It was Thursday; some may know this day as Thanksgiving Day. Up the road lived Aunt Maggie, and she invited TJ over for some Thanksgiving turkey. Thursday, around mid-day, he called his kids from her house to see how they were and to tell them he loved them. He had never been away from them for more than a week.

He helped with the dishes, and they had some coffee and chatted. Soon he headed back to the woods and toward the swamp. Around 2:00 O'clock, he stumbled into Uncle who was out in the Box Stand.

TJ asked how the hunt was going, and Uncle shared that it had been a quiet day. The weather had improved with sunny skies and about 25 degrees, with little wind. Suddenly, a group of 15 deer burst through the nearest tree line and the two hunters shot multiple times, but they missed the deer as they bounded in and out of the tall swamp grass.

Half of the deer escaped to the swamp and the others were headed to a posted property nearby. He stood there disappointed, as he moved to add slugs into his Winchester 1200. He was thinking of what caused those deer to run through so fast, and he quickly thought of the neighbors, and that they must have been doing one of their deer drives.

He thought about what his next move would be, and then he looked back toward the swamp to see if any of those deer were around by chance. He caught a glimpse of movement, and then he could see five heads sticking out of the tall swamp grass.

They must have stopped as they reached the cover and safety of the swamp. They were only about 100 yards away. He surveyed the situation, and he realized they were on a main trail that would meander through the swamp. He quickly thought of a way he could possibly catch up to them and cut them off.

TJ too had learned the terrain of the swamp, and he knew a way to get off a shot. He looked up at the deer again and they began to slowly and cautiously make their way through the swamp. Their attention was focused ahead of them, as if they felt the danger behind them was gone...but it wasn't.

TJ began stalking them. Quietly and calmly. He walked toward another trail that would parallel the trail the deer were on, but it would also give him cover as well. He stopped next to a tree and saw a shooting lane he could use. The swamp grass was still a bit high even though the weight of the snow brought it closer to the ground.

The deer were walking carefully as they headed down a trail that led through the middle of the swamp. Their only mistake was not checking their back trail. They only seemed concerned with what was ahead of them. TJ saw an opening through the grass and bushes and blasted off a shot! Miss!

They stopped. Then kept walking slowly. TJ couldn't believe it. He thought they would have bounded off, but they didn't. The deer resumed their walk through the swamp. He moved straight ahead using bushes and small trees to hide myself. He knew this ground well, so he glided over it.

Eyes ahead and feeling his way with his feet. He was patient, as he realized he had time. The wind was hitting his face, so he knew he wouldn't alert them with his scent. He saw an opening again. A window to the trail where they were walking. He let most of the deer walk through as he had thought the last was the largest. He was correct. The last doe walked through the opening, and he shot. She disappeared in the swamp grass.

He quickly made his way over to the gap he had just shot through moments before, and when he neared the spot, he saw the belly of white fur on the ground.

The chest of the doe was still rising up and down rhythmically. He was next to the deer now, and saw it was still alive, but barely. He knelt a couple of feet away. He looked the deer over and looked at its eyes. A calm look seemed to be on the old doe. He did not want to ruin those final moments of life with the load bang of the shotgun, but he rose to his feet and shouldered the gun and put the sights on the chest of the deer. Before he pulled the trigger, he looked over the deer again, and he watched it take its last breath.

Chapter 12

With a deer on the buck pole, TJ slept in and wanted to get the shack ready for the return of his hunting crew. Father, Pete, and Marlin would be returning to hunt the second weekend of this gun deer season. He wasn't sure when they were coming, but he decided to have a good fire going when they got back to the shack.

As he sat near the woodstove and reached for the match box, he thought the box was on the light side. He shook the box, and then opened it up. He could see they were out of matches to start the woodstove. Of course, something else that isn't going well. He threw the empty box across the shack. It hit the window over the sink and bounced to the cold cement floor. He had not planned for this.

TJ would have to run into the little town nearby to buy some more. As he walked to the truck, he took another hit of whiskey from his flask. He fired up the pick-up truck and backed down the long dirt driveway until he hit the gravel road. He frustratingly hit the gas and spun his tires a bit, and gravel and snow spit from his back end. Town was only a few miles away. He could have just run down and borrowed some from Maggie, but he needed to make another stop anyway.

As he was in the small hardware store, he frustratedly headed to where he might find matches. He turned the corner and noticed a woman walking down the same aisle but toward him. He could tell from afar she was attractive, even with donning a small blaze orange jacket. As they got closer, he could see she was very pretty, and he was a bit taken aback by that.

They both began to smile at one another, as they thought they may simply pass each other, but they both stopped right in front of where the boxes of matches were. He started the conversation. "Can you believe we ran out of matches opening weekend? With a smile. She returned the smile, and glanced over his unshaven, weathered face. "So, did we," She said, and gave a friendly wink and turned and walked away. He was speechless.

He watched her walk away, and as she turned the corner, she gave a quick look back over her shoulder. He didn't seem to know what to do. He forgot what he was doing, and he looked directly at the selection of matches on the shelves. He reached out and grabbed a box of the familiar Diamond Matches that have seemed to inhabit the shack for years on end.

He took the matches, and turned down the aisle, walking fast. As he got to the register, she had just walked out the door. He watched her walk away to an empty pick-up truck. He turned to the cashier and paid for the matches, and he looked to the parking lot and she was gone.

He walked out of the store, and he jumped in his truck. His mood had noticeably changed. He rode back to the shack with a smile on his face. George Straight sang on the radio, and TJ quietly sang along.

His pick-up rolled over the trodden driveway leading to the shack. As he pulled in, he noticed smoke coming out of the chimney. He was confused. He opened the door, and a bit of warmth came over him. Father was sitting in a chair near the wood stove. "Where were you?" he asked.

TJ opened his hand, and the matchbox appeared.

"I went to buy matches!" He yelled gently, with a little smirk.

"We were out!" he added.

"Oh, I had some in this drawer over here." Father said.

TJ laughed abruptly and sat down in grandpa's chair with a little smile on his face.

Father said, "Sorry you had to run into town."

TJ said, "Not a big deal." He looked down at the box of matches in his hand and a small smile came across his face.

TJ went to the woodstove and through another log in.

Later that Friday evening, Pete and Marlin were back up to hunt. TJ had to tell them about his face when they saw him. He felt he gave as good as he got. Pete was furious. His brother got ganged up on and he wasn't there to help. He said, "Let's go to the tavern."

They went. Pete drove. He wasn't going for a drink or to look at deer. He had something else on his mind.

TJ was up for more, and Marlin was along for the ride. They pulled up at the tavern and quickly moved toward the place. Pete led the way, and he opened the door quickly to the old tavern. TJ and Marlin quickly followed. They took a few steps in and scanned the bar.

TJ quietly said. "That's them." He nodded toward a group of men standing on the far side of the bar. Loudly talking and drinking. Instead of three they found a group of five. They must have thought they would be fine in a bigger group. They were mistaken.

Pete moved quickly through the bar area and headed right for the group. As said before, the three of them were sizable men, and not happy. As they approached, TJ was right behind his Pete and TJ slid in front of Pete as they approached the group of men.

He stood facing the group of men and looked at the one who took the cheap shot. His nose was broken, and had white tape over it, and was bruised around it.

"Remember me?" TJ said with anger in his eyes.

The man instantly remembered him. Pete was done holding back. "You the asshole who sucker-punched my brother?"

The man was afraid. Even with his four friends.

Pete without another thought, punched him in the face, and a brawl ensued. Metal bar stools scrapped across the floor and fell to the ground, as men fell to the floor. TJ went immediately after the man who started all the trouble at the bar the other day. He had left the tavern on Wednesday unscathed, but tonight that would not be the case.

Both of the men who were hit, ended up on the floor and were in no hurry to get up. Some pushing and separating took place, between their friends and Marlin. Marlin was in the middle of it, making sure no more cheap shots took place.

Pete and TJ backed up and the owner came over and got between the groups. They stood over the two men, and then looked up at their friends. Ready for more, but more never came. TJ looked at Pete and Marlin and nodded at them. A thank you and a confirmation that that justice was meted out, and they should leave.

A few profanities later, TJ, Pete, and Marlin left the bar, and went back to the truck.

In the truck, TJ looked down at his hand. The knuckles were hurting and a little bloody. He clenched his fist and released it, and he looked out the truck window into the darkness as his Pete drove away from the tavern down the cold, dark road.

They got back to the shack, and father was there.

"Where you boys been?" father said.

They looked at each other.

"Just stopped at the tavern," Pete said.

"Ready for poker?"

The brothers looked at each other and smiled a little. TJ walked over to his bunk, and he sat down for a moment. He didn't really need to hit that guy. *I guess he had it coming.*

He eventually joined the others at the table, and Pete had a glass of whiskey ready for him. TJ never drank a drop that night.

Chapter 13

After a quiet morning, at mid-day TJ found himself in the heart of the property. He had been in the Swamp-stand trying to cover several trails in the middle of the swamp. Twice that morning a group of does had come by about 80 yards behind him, but there was only one small shooting lane, and he had taken a shot and missed.

Frustrated, he realized the deer would continue to use this escape trail throughout the weekend, so he decided to change things up even though it meant getting down from his stand. He decided to walk towards that trail and clear a new shooting lane that would give me better visual access to that trail from his tree stand and offer him a closer shot the next time deer would come through.

Generally, if you stay on stand long enough in this area, you will have an opportunity at a deer, but he decided to change his own luck or at least try to put the odds in his favor. He climbed down the wooden tree-stand, and it moaned and creaked.

TJ stepped to the ground and he walked over toward the trail and began breaking branches on a small tree that was blocking a possible shooting lane. He wanted to make quick work of it, so he did not try to do this in any quiet fashion.

The branches cracked and snapped in the cold Wisconsin weather, and after a minute or so of this, he looked around. TJ then decided simply to stand near the trail with the little tree and swamp grass as cover, instead of going back to the tree stand.

Almost immediately, he heard something from behind him. It was the unmistaken sound of a deer moving through the swamp. He turned his head slowly to see a large, dark rack seemingly floating through the swamp grass 50 yards away. TJ froze.

He was standing on the ground, and the heavy-racked 9-pointer was headed his way, but his gun was held in a manner that it was pointed away from the oncoming deer. The buck stopped and the rack was silhouetted by the late afternoon November sun. A beautiful sight. The buck was 30 yards away, and it began moving again down the trail that would come right to TJ. He waited anxiously. Not sure what to do. He kept looking at it over his right shoulder.

The buck was almost on top of him at about 10 yards. With a quick swing to his right, the Winchester was at his shoulder. The buck jumped to its left, with his eye looking right at TJ. It was bounding broadside to TJ's location now on the ground, next to a straggly tree. As he quickly eyed up the buck in his iron sights, he squeezed the trigger. The loud "Bang" of the shotgun echoed through the swamp.

The buck came to a stop and stood at 30 yards quartering away. It just stood there. TJ could see a dark stained area on its side, as he was frantically trying to remove the jammed empty shell from his 12-gauge pump shotgun. He looked at the buck and then back down at this gun trying to unjam the spent shell from the action of the shotgun. He looked up again, worried the buck would head for the neighboring property.

The buck, still standing in the same spot, wavered from left to right, and then right to left. Then it simply fell over. He stood there in disbelief. The big buck was down. No second shot would be needed. As he stood near the buck now, he was in awe. He stopped fumbling with his gun, and he began walking toward the downed animal. He stood and looked it over. *Dark rack. 9 points. Thick antlers.* It was the buck. He knelt and put his hand on the shoulder of the dead buck, and he handled the antlers with awe. He was thankful toward the buck. A slight feeling of remorse came and went, as he knew this is part of the hunt.

He heard a sound ahead of him, and as he looked up, he saw Ol' Hutch walk into the opening where the buck fell. A big smile came from his grizzled face, and he walked over to TJ and shook his hand.

"That is the biggest buck I've seen in years out here," Ol'Hutch stated with a gravely voice.

"I believe you are right,' TJ said proudly with a nod. TJ shared the story of getting the buck, and Ol'Hutch listened intently.

Soon TJ saw Pete and Marlin approaching.

After Pete and Marlin helped him get the buck back to the shack, they tied it up to the buck pole. TJ proudly looked it over again. Uncle would later confirm it was the one he saw in the field the night before opening day.

Chapter 14

Sunday morning had come and TJ with two deer on the deer pole had decided to sleep in. He woke up shortly after first light, and the other hunters had already left for their stands. He awoke slowly, enjoying simply laying in his bunk and thinking about his week at deer camp. It was a crazy week, but all had worked out, and he felt happy.

He slid out of his sleeping bag as the sun was truly up in the East, and he walked over to the wood stove. He instinctively placed the old newspaper in, then the kindling, and reached for the matches. He grabbed the box of matches, and noticed it was the box he picked up the other day at the store.

He thought back to that Friday morning, and the small chat he had with the woman he had met. He smiled a little smile. He wondered if he would see her again. He continued to make the fire, and then closed the steel door and made his way to the coffee pot.

While he had taken the buck, and had a good week at camp, he found himself out there one last time. They had other tags that were still not filled as that day they were group hunting. He went back to the creek bottom for this evening hunt, in which he did not use the Tree Bridge, with Pete not far away.

It was not going to be about tagging another deer, but to simply to be out in the woods one more time. He only would be hunting the last hour and a half of the day, but any time spent surrounded by trees, the critters, the flowing creek, and a setting sun are always a good reason to be on stand he thought.

TJ looked around the creek bottom. The sun was an inch from the tops of the trees, a partly sunny day was a perfect way to end the week. The temperature was fair today, no stinging cold, but a cool 20 degrees with a little wind. Perched in his wooden ladder stand near the creek bottom, nestled in a big maple with multiple trunks shooting out from the ground, he again scanned the area. A large grey squirrel was making its way along a fallen tree, and the pair of wood ducks were noisily splashing in a bend of the creek looking for food.

Some thoughts were going through his head. Good thoughts, which have not happened in a while. He missed his children, and was looking forward to seeing them, and sharing his new stories with them. He thought about the future with more optimism than usual, and he wondered if he would ever see her again.

The shadows of the trees grew longer. The sun was now almost behind the them, and he caught a glimpse of movement a hundred yards away. He saw a young buck move out of the thick coverage of the creek bottom and make its way up the bank. It was moving cautiously and stopped to check the wind. A week after being chased all over the woods, this little buck had grown wise. It was now 75 yards away, and it was walking down the edge of the wood.

TJ tightened his grip on his Winchester, which seemed to be an involuntary motion after over 25 years of hunting. He had no intention to shoot. The buck was moving closer, and finally stopped at about 50 yards. The buck checked the wind, and it looked back toward the creek bottom and seemed to look TJ's way. It sat and stared for a moment, and then with the setting sun made its way toward a cut corn field.

TJ simply smiled and watched the cornfield for a few moments, and then the sun set at deer camp.

About the Author

Thomas A Fischer is an avid outdoorsman who spends his time hunting, fishing, camping, hiking, reading and writing. While Wisconsin has been home to most of his outdoor experiences, he has pursued adventures throughout the Western United States, Canada, and Alaska. A father of four, and an educator of over 20 years, he has now taken his first steps into published writing. Thomas resides outside of Madison, WI.